MW01618169

POND
PUMPKIN PATCH
STRAWBERRY PATCH
APPLE TREES
N
W
E
S
LETTUCE PATCH

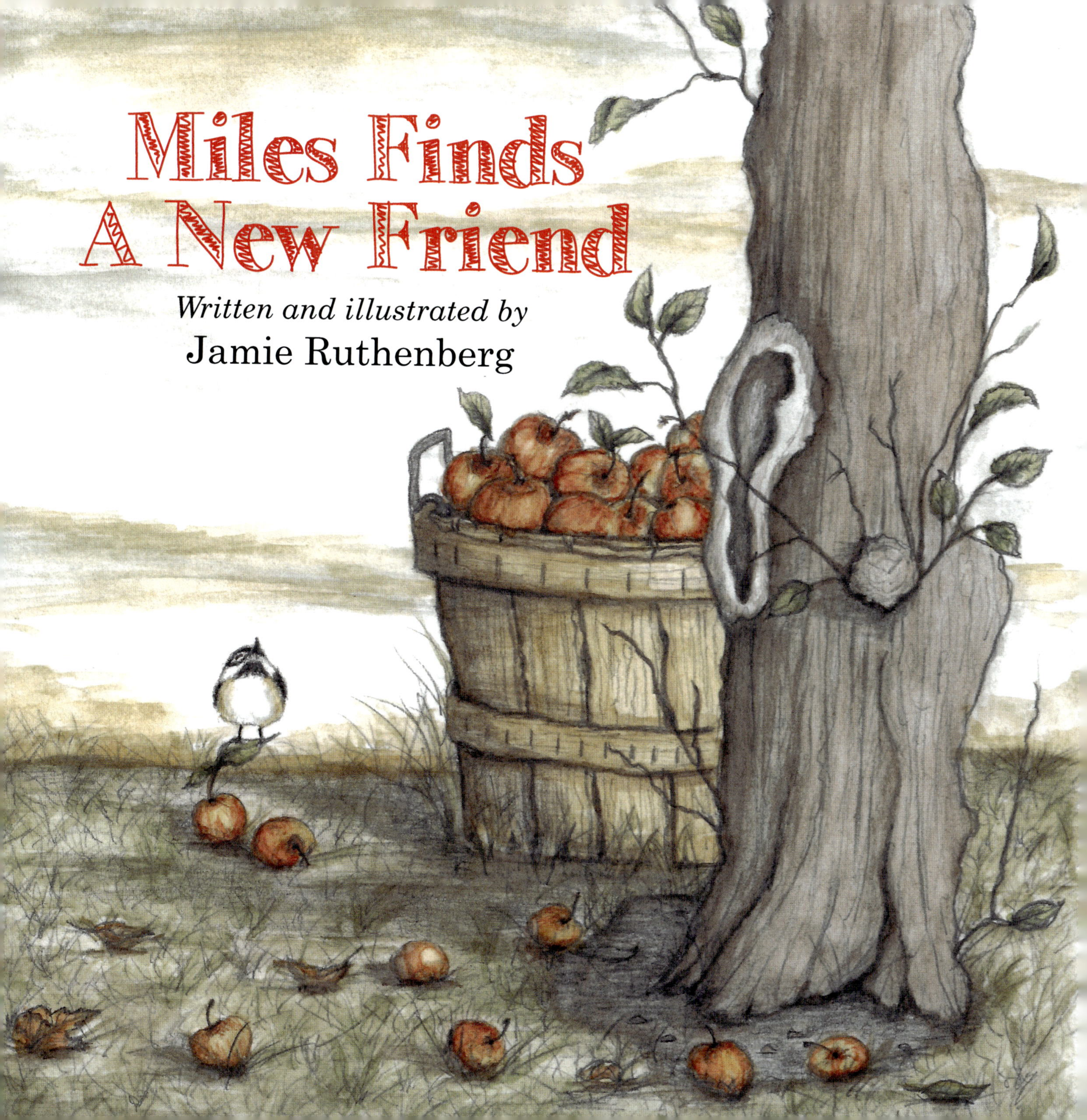
Miles Finds
A New Friend
Written and illustrated by
Jamie Ruthenberg

Published by J. Ruthenberg and Co. Writing Services, Inc.

ISBN-13: 978-0578423173

ISBN-10: 0578423170

For the child
who shows kindness
to those who need
it most

Miles could smell a hint of burning leaves in the crisp morning air as he and his mother worked in the pumpkin patch. It was finally time for the autumn harvest, when all of the pumpkins and apples needed to be picked and put into big bushels.

As he picked another sugar pumpkin, Miles could not help but feel excited about the party his mother hosted every fall for their close friends and neighbors to celebrate the autumn harvest. There were only a few more days to prepare and so much to do!

Miles stopped a moment to look out at the pond that was surrounded by golden oaks and deep red maples. Their turned leaves were bold against the sky's low clouds.

Miles' mother carried bushel after bushel of apples while Miles pulled the big wooden wagon, filled with pumpkins of all sizes and shapes.

Every year, when the kitchen was packed with what they picked, Miles' mother would set aside what she knew they needed. Then Miles would help her sort through what was left to share with all of their neighbors.

The neighbors especially looked forward to his mother's apples, for they made the most delicious pies.

The next day, Miles delivered big baskets of tasty treats to the neighborhood, including Charlie's house, his good friend from school.

After handing him the basket, Miles said, "I only have one house left. My Mama said new neighbors live there. Would you like to come with me?"

"Sure!" said Charlie and, after he asked his mother, off they went.

Miles pulled the wagon as they made their way to the new neighbors' house. They stepped onto the porch and knocked on the door. When the door opened, they were surprised to see Henrik, the new student in their class at school.

"I am Miles and this is Charlie from school. I didn't realize we are neighbors," Miles said with a smile as he gave Henrik the basket. "This is a gift from my Mama's garden to your family to celebrate the fall harvest. The apples are especially good this year!"

"Thank you," Henrik said with smiling eyes.

After saying goodbye to Henrik, Miles walked Charlie back to his house.

“Henrik doesn’t talk much in school, and he looks kind of sad and lonely,” Charlie said as they walked. “He is taller then the other kids in our class. No one really talks to him.”

Miles thought a moment. “Just because he’s taller or quiet doesn’t mean he is not a good person. I wouldn’t have had anything to eat for lunch yesterday if it were not for him.”

Charlie looked confused.

“My sandwich fell out of my bag earlier that day. He picked it up and made sure I got it back before lunch,” Miles said with a smile.

"I heard he helped Violet's little brother last weekend," said Charlie.

"Really?" asked Miles.

"Yep. I guess Gabe was climbing a tree and was too scared to come down. Henrik ran over, climbed right up, and helped him down, just like that."

"Hey, there's nothing in your wagon!" Charlie suddenly realized. "Miles, will you pull me if I get in it?"

"Sure!" Miles said as he laughed. Charlie lay with a lazy smile as Miles pulled him the rest of the way home.

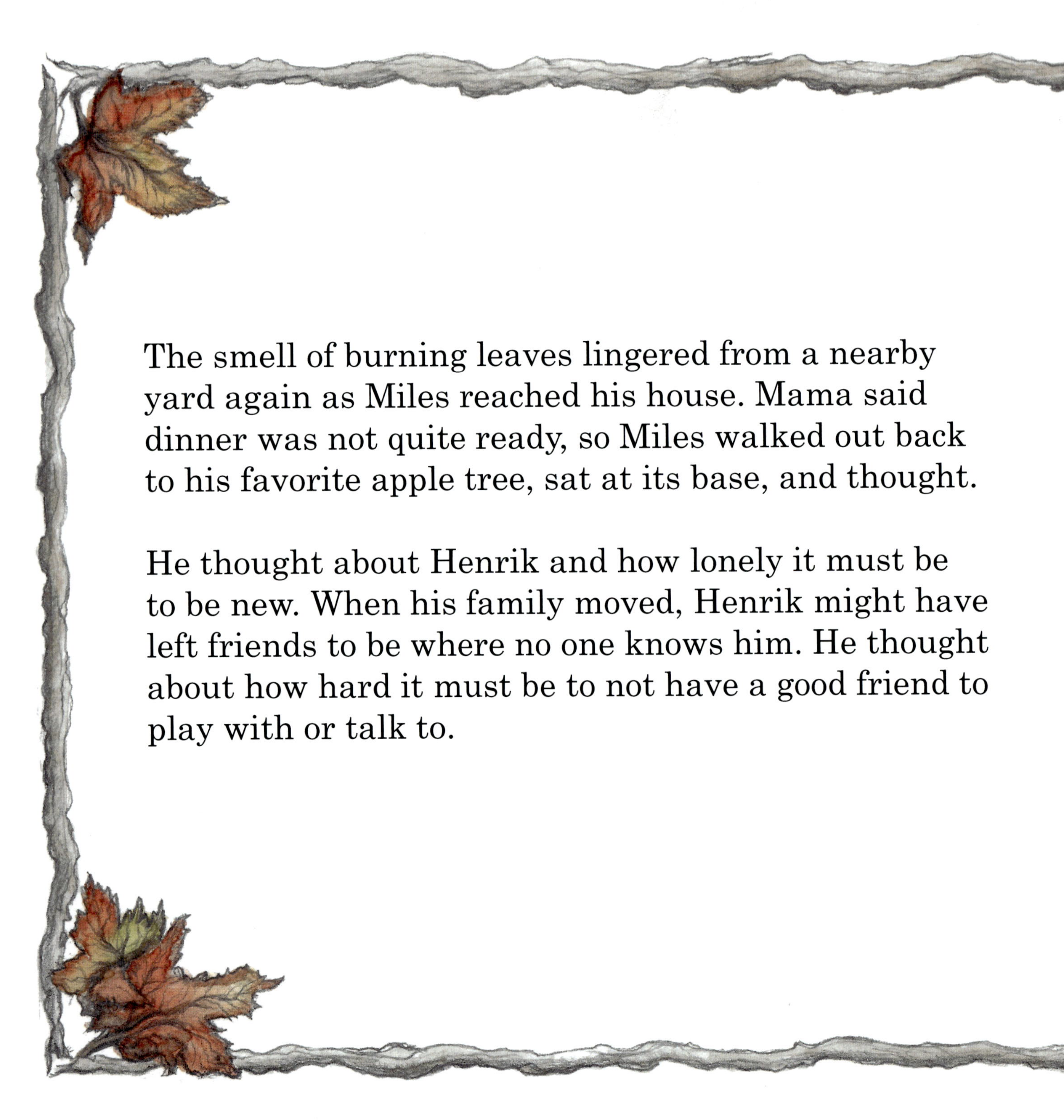

The smell of burning leaves lingered from a nearby yard again as Miles reached his house. Mama said dinner was not quite ready, so Miles walked out back to his favorite apple tree, sat at its base, and thought.

He thought about Henrik and how lonely it must be to be new. When his family moved, Henrik might have left friends to be where no one knows him. He thought about how hard it must be to not have a good friend to play with or talk to.

"Henrik will have a good friend,"
Miles said to himself.

"Me."

At that moment…

Miles had an idea.

After dinner that night, Miles got out his best paper, his special pencil, and his watercolor paints, and he made a card to invite Henrik to the yearly harvest party. His mother sent an invitation to his family, but Miles wanted to send one especially to Henrik.

Hi Henrik,

You are invited to the yearly autumn harvest party!

Day: Tommorow

Time: 3:00 p.m.

Place: My house

I will be wearing a costume and so will many of my friends, so if you want to wear one, feel free! There will be fall treats and fun games. I really hope to see you!

Your friend,
Miles

The next day, Miles walked to Henrik's house and knocked on the door. When Henrik answered, Miles handed him the homemade card.

"This is for you," said Miles.

As Henrik read the card, his face lit up. "I will be there," he said, smiling. "Thank you, Miles. I wouldn't miss it!"

Miles couldn't help but smell something wonderful filling the air from the front door. He stuck his nose up to take in the warm scent.

Henrik chuckled and said, "My mom is making apple pies with the apples you gave us. We are bringing some of them to the party tomorrow. It's my job to peel all the apples and I have a lot more to do."

"Hey, would you like to help?"

The glow from the fireplace and the oven warmed the kitchen. Miles stood on a stool and helped Henrik peel apple after apple while Henrik's mother rolled mounds of homemade dough. Miles watched as she then mixed warm spices and vanilla into a big bowl of thick cream to pour over the apples.

"This is my Mom's homemade apples and cream pie."

Henrik's mother looked at Miles with a promising smile and said, "Once you taste this pie, you will never forget it."

Vanilla

The following day, it was finally time for the big party! Miles' home was filled with the chatting and laughter of friends and neighbors as they nibbled on their favorite autumn dishes they brought to share. The smell of warm spices and seasonal soups and stews made Miles' mouth water.

When it came time, he could barely wait to taste the apples and cream pie Henrik's mother made the night before.

"I am so thankful for your mother's apples this year. They made the pies the best they have ever been!" Henrik's mother said as she cut into the pies and passed out thick slices.

After his first bite, Miles hoped for at least two more pieces! It was truly unforgetable, as was this day with his friends, old and new.

FIRE
CHIEF
MAIL

FIRE
CHIEF

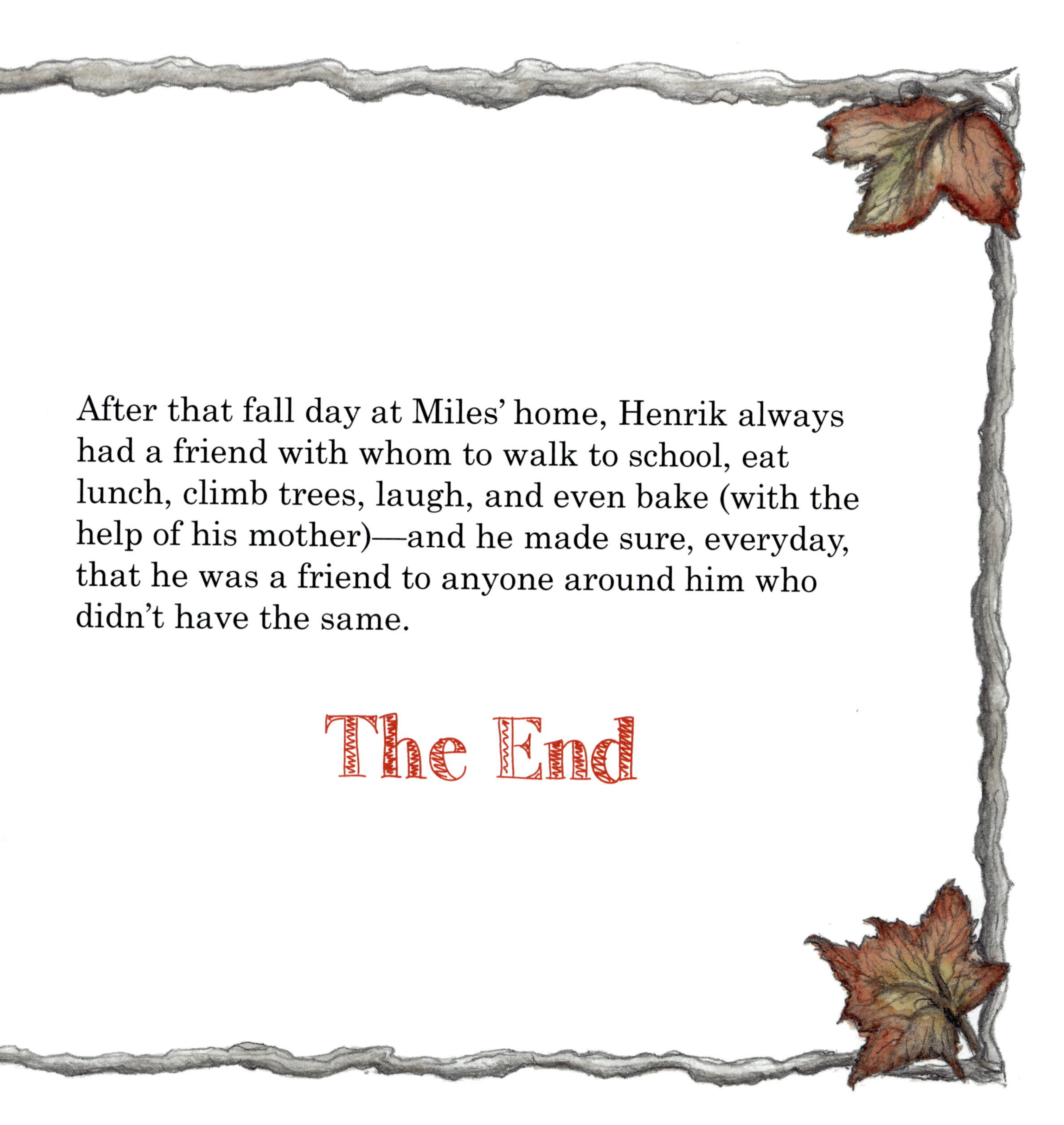

After that fall day at Miles' home, Henrik always had a friend with whom to walk to school, eat lunch, climb trees, laugh, and even bake (with the help of his mother)—and he made sure, everyday, that he was a friend to anyone around him who didn't have the same.

The End

Hi there!

I am writing a letter again, my friend, because I really love to hear what you think!

- Did something like this ever happen to you? What happened?
- Have you ever felt like I did in the story, or like Henrik? What were your feelings and why?

Sometimes stories are like other stories.

- Did you ever read a story like this one?
- What was the story? How are they alike?

I hope you write me back soon! I love hearing from you!

Your Friend,
Miles

For the teachers, parents, and adults using this book:

As I have mentioned in the previous books, fostering a love for storytelling and reading is critically important for the children in our lives, and making connections to stories is equally important and may help increase comprehension levels. Among many teaching points, **this book focuses on text-to-self and text-to-text connections**, which are terms for making personal connections to a story as well as recognizing similarities between two stories. ***Miles Finds a New Friend* may be used to introduce and practice the idea of making these connections, as Miles personally discusses the two topics with his readers at the end of the story.**

For further discussion points, this book can also be grouped with other books based on the following themes, many of which could be gathered together under one main theme, **treating others as you would want to be treated:**

empathy and compassion
helping others/charity
seeking to understand
friendship
comfort and family
thinking before acting
respecting others
generosity
peaceful problem solving

For writing activities, one may use this book to introduce and practice **letter writing.**

My Personal Connection to *Miles Finds a New Friend*

When I was in fourth grade, my family moved out of Detroit and into a newly built, little home in a new nearby town. They were so excited to be moving out of that old, cramped duplex; I, however, was devastated. I didn't want to leave because I truly loved the people in my school and all of my friends in the neighborhood where we lived. If you have ever moved away from a school you loved, you know how I felt on my last day when I watched out the window of my mother's car as she drove me away.

Days after, I found myself standing in front of an entire class of unfamiliar faces. The room was quiet as they all sat in their desks and stared at me.

"Meet our new student, Jamie Ruthenberg," the teacher said with a smile. I remember hearing one of the boys in the back of the class sigh and say under his breath, "Oh no, not another girl." That line makes me chuckle now, but it didn't then.

I was "the new kid," as we often call it, just like Henrik. Being a bit shy at the time, I kept quietly to myself for several days as other children talked and laughed with each other. There were two or three kids in particular who weren't always very nice, poking fun that I was quiet and that I was taller than many of the other students.

Most importantly, one day stands out in my mind. It was an early spring day and my class was told to line up for recess. Students rushed from all ends of the room into line. One of the "not-so-nice" kids was standing behind me in line as another student, who had poked fun at me earlier, kindly asked if she could be in front of me. I nodded and smiled, and moved back a bit so she could fit in line. Now, I knew she was "taking cuts," as we called it, but I also knew from overhearing her talk earlier that she was in a hurry and I wanted to help.

"Why are you so nice?" the girl behind me said, with a disapproving frown. At nine years old, I didn't know what to say to her standing there that day, so I didn't say anything at all. Looking back at that moment so many years later, I now know how to answer her question.

It's easy to be kind to those who are always kind as well. However, a person with true integrity and compassion will find it in his or her heart to be kind to those who have not always done the same in the past. Treating others as you would want to be treated—which Miles does throughout his stories—means being respectful, understanding, helpful, and empathetic to those who maybe weren't always their best selves.

It also means being a friend to those who need one most. Miles understood this with Henrik, and so did another student that spring day on the playground who smiled and asked if I wanted to swing with her and her friends. Suddenly, from that day on, school wasn't lonely anymore, and I wasn't "the new kid." I was Jamie.

—Jamie Ruthenberg

About the Author

Jamie Ruthenberg is a Detroit-born author and artist, as well as a professional writer. Along with writing and illustrating *The Miles Series,* she is also the illustrator of the *Pincy's Auto Show Adventures Series* supported by the North American International Auto Show and PNC. The series is a not-for-profit collaborative effort to help preschool children succeed in school and in life. Moreover, Jamie is also the illustrator of the book *The Tale of the Beautiful Cat*, written by the late Ruth Cain, a true advocate of childhood literacy in the Detroit Public Schools.

by Jamie Ruthenberg

AUTHOR / ILLUSTRATOR

In addition to her career as an author and self-taught artist, Jamie is also a writer in many different genres as owner of J. Ruthenberg & Co. Writing Services, Inc., a professional business writing, creative writing, and editing company.

Her educational past includes two Bachelor's degrees and a Master's of Art Degree, with majors centering on English, creative writing, English composition, and elementary education. She has taught the beauty of the writing and art process to students in a wide range of classrooms, from graduate students to kindergarteners, and has published various works of fiction, nonfiction, poetry, and visual art.

Among her works, *The Miles Series* is one of the closest to her heart, for Jamie has been sketching the character of Miles since she was a small child. Many years later, with watercolor and pencil, she has developed him into a kindhearted and thoughtful soul that treats other with love and respect, even during challenging circumstances. He is truly a character with integrity who treats others as he would want to be treated.

Today Jamie lives in Clarkston, Michigan with her daughter, Grace, and their two cats, Oz and Ella.

“Don’t become preoccupied with
your child’s academic ability
but instead
teach them to sit with those sitting alone.
Teach them to be kind.
Teach them to offer their help.
Teach them to be a friend to the lonely.
Teach them to encourage others.
Teach them to think about other people.
Teach them to share.
Teach them to look for the good.

This is how they will change the world.”

~Unknown

Artist's note:

The paintings for this book were created with pencil and watercolor.
The text was set in Century Schoolbook.

If you enjoyed this book by Jamie Ruthenberg, you and your family may also enjoy the first three books in this delightful series.

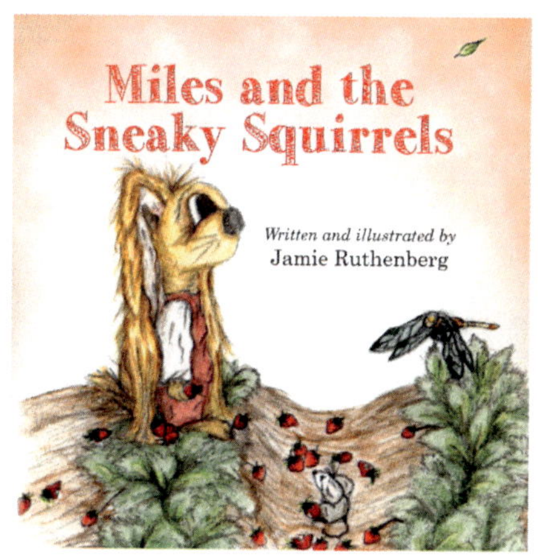

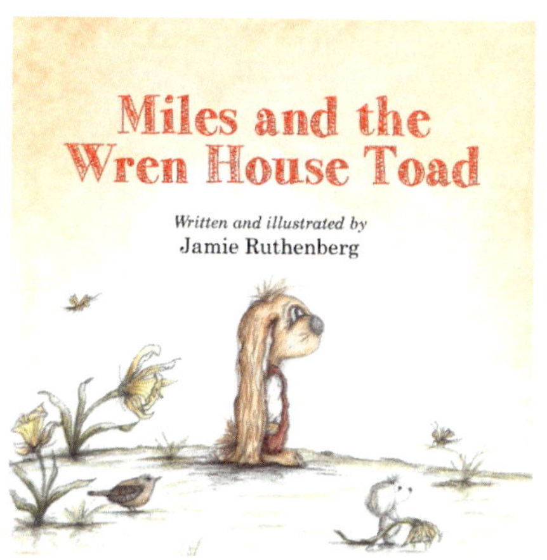

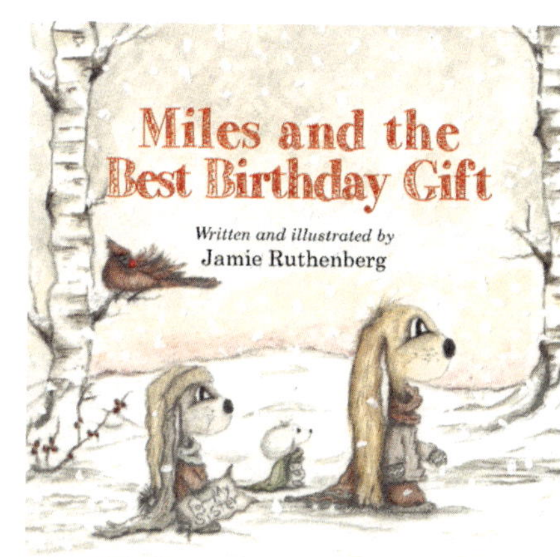

Miles and the Sneaky Squirrels Paperback ISBN: 978-0692486054
Miles and the Wren House Toad Paperback ISBN: 978-0692704509
Miles and the Best Birthday Gift Paperback ISBN:978-0692896143

Signed copies available for purchase at:
JamieRuthenberg.com